A WOODLAND MYSTERY™

The Secret of the Old Oak Trunk

A WOODLAND MYSTERY
By Irene Schultz

The Wright Group®

To my mother, who let me read to
her when I was young

The Secret of the Old Oak Trunk
©1996 Wright Group Publishing, Inc.
©1996 Story by Irene Schultz
Cover and cameo illustrations by Taylor Bruce
Interior illustrations by Meredith Yasui
Map illustration by Alicia Kramer

Woodland Mysteries™
© Wright Group Publishing, Inc.

The Woodland Mysteries were created by the
Wright Group development team.

The Wright Group
19201 120th Avenue NE
Bothell, WA 98011

Printed in the United States of America

10 9 8 7 6 5

ISBN: 0-7802-7227-7

What family solves mysteries...has adventures all over the world...and loves oatmeal cookies?

It's the Woodlanders!

Sammy Westburg (10 years old)
His sister Kathy Westburg (13)
His brother Bill Westburg (14)
His best friend Dave Briggs (16)
His best grown-up friend Mrs. Tandy
And Mop, their little dog!

The children all lost their parents, but with Mrs. Tandy have made their own family.

Why are they called the Woodlanders? Because they live in a big house in the Bluff Lake woods. On Woodland Street!

Together they find fun, mystery, and adventure. What are they up to now?

Read on!

Meet the Woodlanders!

Sammy Westburg
Sammy is a ten-year-old wonder! He's big for his fifth-grade class, and big-mouthed, too. He has wild hair and makes awful spider faces. Even so, you can't help liking him.

Bill Westburg
Bill, fourteen, is friendly and strong, and only one inch taller than his brother Sammy. He loves Sammy, but pokes him to make him be quiet! He's in junior high.

Kathy Westburg
Kathy, thirteen, is small, shy, and smart. She wants to be a doctor some day! She loves to be with Dave, and her brothers kid her about it. She's in junior high, too.

Dave Briggs

Dave, sixteen, is tall and blond. He can't walk, so he uses a wheelchair and drives a special car. He likes coaching high-school sports, solving mysteries, and reading. And Kathy!

Mrs. Tandy

Sometimes the kids call her Mrs. T. She's Becky Tandy, their tall, thin, caring friend. She's always ready for a new adventure, and for making cookies!

Mop

Mop is the family's little tan dog. Sometimes they have to leave him behind with friends. But he'd much rather be running after Sammy.

Table of Contents

Chapter 1:
The Falling Book

SLAM!

Ten-year-old Sammy Westburg jumped straight up out of his chair at the library.

He said, "WHAT DID YOU DO, BILL?"

His brother Bill, fourteen, said, "Nothing! I didn't do anything!"

The sudden noise had made Kathy, their thirteen-year-old sister, drop her pencil!

Sammy, Bill, and Kathy were with sixteen-year-old Dave Briggs and Mrs. Tandy.

The five of them, the Woodlanders, were the only ones in the Bluff Lake library's Garden Room.

It was always quiet there ... until the slam, that is.

Dave and Mrs. Tandy looked around in every direction.

Then Dave pointed across the room.

The others turned to see what he was pointing at.

A huge book lay on the floor.

Sammy looked worried. He said,

"Boy, wait until Mrs. Moore sees what happened! She's going to be SO MAD!

"Librarians can't STAND it when the books are messed up!"

Kathy whispered, "But we didn't knock it down ... I hope she doesn't think we did it!

"Do you think she even heard the noise?   Is anyone coming down the hall?"

Dave said, "Don't worry, Kathy.   She knows we wouldn't hurt anything on purpose.

"Let's go see if that book's OK."

He rolled his wheelchair across the room.

The others followed him.

The five of them formed a circle around the fallen book.

Bill said, "Look, it fell with its pages open."

Mrs. Tandy said, "My, it looks really old."

Sammy frowned. "Do you think it's torn? Can we pick it up?"

Bill said, "It looks all right to me. Here, I'll get it."

He gently lifted the heavy old book. He placed it, still open, on a table.

Kathy stared at the open pages. She said, "Hey, I think it looks like a plan for a garden!"

Bill lifted the cover a little so he could look at it.

He said, "The book is called *Old*

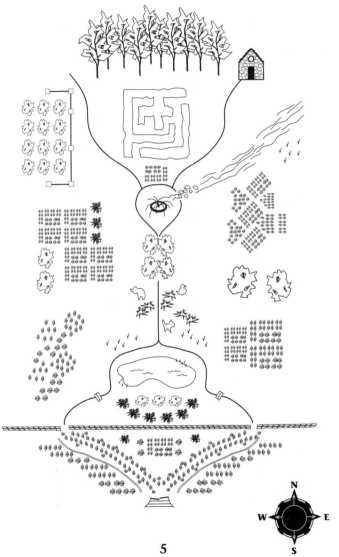

5

English Gardens.

"You're right, Kathy, it's the plan of a garden. And boy, is it a big one!"

Dave said, "Not big, HUGE!

"Look, its length is written here. It's just about as long as a football field.

"And it's almost as wide as it is long!"

Mrs. Tandy touched the page. She said, "Look at the tiny words printed all over it."

Sammy tried to sound out some of them. "Hep-at-i-ca ... wis-ter-i-a. Wait a little minute! I think it's a secret code!"

Mrs. Tandy laughed. "Sammy, you're always looking for mysteries. Those are just the names of flowers."

Kathy said, "Look at all the tiny drawings.

"One's a wavy little stream.

"And these must be stepping-stones."

Dave said, "And see? This part of the

drawing looks like a maze of tall bushes!"

Sammy pointed. "What's this little house way down here? Maybe it's a doghouse. What do you think, Bill?"

Bill said, "I can't guess what it is, Sammy. I'm too busy trying to figure out something else.

"What made this book fall off the shelf in the first place?"

Chapter 2:
The English Garden

Dave rubbed his head in thought.

He said, "What DID make this book fall on the floor? Did one of you hear a truck go by?

"Sometimes traffic makes things shake around and fall."

Mrs. Tandy shook her head. "I don't remember any loud traffic sounds."

Bill looked at the shelf where the old book had stood.

He said, "Well, this metal bookend was holding it against the other books. But now the bookend is pushed aside."

Kathy said, "The book's probably been leaning too hard against it for a long time ... and it pushed heavier and heavier the more it leaned.

"Finally the bookend just slid away and the book fell over."

Sammy said, "Bill, don't laugh or I'll punch you. But it just seems funny that the book fell for no reason. So maybe there IS a reason."

But Bill said, "I'm not laughing, Sammy. I almost had the feeling that the book tried to get us to notice it. But I know that's stupid."

Mrs. Tandy looked excited. "Well, it sure caught MY attention ... and it made me wonder where this garden was ... and if it's still there.

"I even wish I could go see it.

"Exactly where in England is it, Dave?"

Dave said, "Look what it says on the next page. You wouldn't even HAVE to go to England.

"It says here this English garden was copied in the United States in 1860.

"Let's see, that was a year before the Civil War began.

"The garden was planted by a man named Benson. Thomas Benson. He was from England."

Dave looked up. "There's more. It says he settled in southern Indiana near a town called Enid.

"Then he planted a garden exactly like this English one.

"But a couple of years later, during the Civil War, he made a new plan for the cutting garden part.

"And here's Thomas Benson's cutting garden plan!"

Sammy said, "Great, but what's a cutting garden?"

Kathy said, "It's when you grow flowers to cut and put in vases."

Mrs. Tandy said, "My, doesn't that seem strange?

"In the middle of a terrible war … there he was thinking about where to grow the flowers for the house!"

Dave said, "It says here that he left the new plan for his wife. But both of them died before it was carried out.

"It says his children planted the new

cutting garden in 1870. That was five years after the war ended."

Kathy looked over Dave's shoulder. She pointed to a sentence.

In a quiet, dreamy voice she read it aloud. "The garden can be seen to this very day."

Then shyly she asked, "What about our spring vacation next week? Do we have any plans for it?"

Bill said, "Hmm ... this book was printed in 1900. You don't really think this garden would still be there, do you? All these years later?

"Probably not a chance."

Suddenly Sammy said, "I don't care what you say, Bill!

"I bet it IS still there!

"I KNOW it's still there!

"In fact, it's practically BEGGING us to drive down and see it. Let's go!"

Dave smiled and said, "It would be easy enough to drive there.

"In fact, it would only take about twelve hours, steady driving.

"Mrs. T. and I could take turns with my car and drive right through."

Mrs. Tandy said, "I do love to drive

14

your station wagon, Dave. The hand controls seem so much easier than foot pedals."

Bill said, "Well, I guess a falling book is a weird reason to take a trip. But I think it's a good idea anyway."

Dave said, "That settles it. We all want to go. I'll go copy this garden plan right now.

"Then we can study it on the drive."

Bill said, "Make a copy for each of us, will you? And make copies of the new cutting garden plan, too!"

Sammy was so excited, he grabbed Bill's arms.

He danced a little dance and spun him around.

He sang, "We get to go to the garden, we get to go to the garden."

Then Bill added, "Our plan began to harden."

And Sammy squealed, "Oops, I beg your pardon," and pinched Bill. He ducked around a table so Bill couldn't pinch him back.

He danced all around the room.

Suddenly a mad-looking face appeared in the doorway!

Uh-oh! It was Mrs. Moore, the librarian.

She growled, "What's all the noise in here?"

Then she saw it was the Woodlanders. "Why, hello, Becky Tandy! Hello, kids! What in the world is happening here?"

Bill said, "I'm sorry we forgot to be quiet. We got so excited."

Mrs. Moore noticed the big open book on the table.

She said, "My, I had no idea that this book was so exciting."

They told her about its mysterious fall from the shelf.

Mrs. Tandy added, "And we've decided to go down to Indiana. We are going to visit that garden ... if there still is a garden."

Sammy said, "Hey, we better get going!

"There are only four days left until Saturday!

"That's only four afternoons and nights to pack.

"Now, what should I take?"

17

Chapter 3:
Aren't We There Yet?

So Sammy packed ...
    100 pieces of bubble gum
    a compass
    his pocketknife

a ball of string

twenty marbles

a box of rubber bands

a little chessboard

little chess pieces

fish hooks

fishing floats

a mystery book

a number-square puzzle

a pencil box

a spiral notebook

Bill's colored markers (He couldn't find his, so he figured good old Bill wouldn't mind.)

eleven comic books

five apples

... and an extra pair of shoes.

And those were just the things he took in a shopping bag.

By 7:00 Saturday morning he also had a huge suitcase stuffed full.

The others had packed four small suitcases ... one per person. They loaded them into the station wagon.

Then Bill put a shopping bag on the floor of the back seat.

Dave lifted himself from his chair into the driver's seat. Kathy got in next to him.

Mop, their little tan dog, jumped onto her lap. When she closed the door, he rested his front paws on the window and looked out happily.

Bill and Sammy put Dave's wheelchair into the back of the wagon. Then they got into the back seat with Mrs. Tandy.

Mop began to bark and jump up and down on Kathy's lap.

Sammy called, "Mop says he's ready! Let's go!"

Dave started the car.

The first thing Sammy did was snoop

into Bill's shopping bag.

He found pencils and paper and ...
ten cold baked potatoes
crunchy fried lima beans
a book about games for the car
a bag of carrot sticks and celery
a loaf of sliced bran bread
a big chunk of sliced baloney
a bag of pears
a bag of lettuce
fifteen hard-boiled eggs
paper cups and plastic spoons
mustard
salt and pepper shakers
... and dry food for Mop.

He said, "You should see the good stuff I took, Bill. Why did you bring those terrible cold potatoes?"

Bill said, "For lunch. Or dinner. They're good cold with salt and pepper. I had them that way in Scouts once."

22

Sammy shrieked, "YUCK!"

He grabbed his nose with one hand and his stomach with the other.

He fell to the side and pretended to die on Bill's lap.

Bill tickled him.   That brought him back to life FAST.

Then Bill groaned, "Well, I see this might be a long trip, traveling with you, Sammy. Time to start a game.

"Here's a pencil and some paper. Now watch the road signs. Try to find words for every letter in the alphabet, starting with A."

Just when he said that, Bill saw a sign that said: HOME COOKING AND HOME-MADE BREAD.

He said, "I've got A, B, and C. There's AND and BREAD and COOKING, right on that sign!"

Sammy said, "That's no fair. That's cheating!

"You only saw ONE sign and you've practically got the whole alphabet!"

Bill said, "Well, we can make a new rule if you feel that way. Only one word from each sign."

Sammy nodded. "That's better."

Then he saw a sign that said:

He shouted, "No, we have to play the old way, Bill! And I've got D and E and F and G and H. That NEW rule you made up is cheating."

25

Bill said, "Sammy, you're making me MAD!"

Dave said, "Looks like we need a new game. Let's look for license plates from other states."

So they played that for about twenty minutes.

Then Sammy said, "Aren't we there yet? We've been driving all day already!

"Maybe we should eat to give us strength."

He passed out his apples and bubble gum.

They played more car games ... and they counted twenty-two signs for home cooking, and eleven for all-night truck repairs.

Then Sammy said, "Aren't we there yet? We've been driving a week!"

They played Twenty Questions. They read all the comic books.

Then Sammy said, "Aren't we there yet? We've been driving a month!"

They stopped to get gas, and to use the restrooms, and to walk Mop.

They ate potatoes (Sammy ate the three biggest ones, after all) … and eggs … and celery … and carrot sticks … and crunchy lima beans.

Then Sammy said, "Aren't we there yet? We've been driving a year!"

They played chess until Mop jumped into the back seat and sent the chess pieces flying. So Sammy read part of his mystery book.

Then he said, "Aren't we there yet? We've been driving a thousand years!"

They ate baloney and lettuce sandwiches … and finished the celery and carrot sticks, and ate all the pears.

Then Sammy said, "Aren't we there yet? We've been driving for about a thousand light years."

Finally it was 7:00 at night. Sammy looked at the road map and then out the window.

He said, "HEY! We ARE almost there! And look, here's a motel!"

They rented a big room where they could all sleep.

They were so tired they fell into bed.

Sammy said, "Boy, we've driven forEVER.

"My back aches. My jaws are tired. I've got a wad of bubble gum stuck in my hair. I ate three of those disGUSTing cold potatoes.

"Four of my chess pieces are lost. And Mop is sleeping on my stomach, so now I can't turn over.

"Some trip! That garden better BE there!"

Chapter 4: A Hermit

"Bring out your suitcases. Into the car, guys!"

Morning had come. Bill was trying to get them to hurry.

Sammy was wearing his Superman T-shirt. Still, he looked glum.

He said, "Thirty miles to go for breakfast. The motel man said we have to drive all the way to Enid for a meal.

"And how come he didn't know anything about the garden? What if it's not there anymore?"

Mrs. Tandy said, "I wouldn't worry too much about him, honey. Maybe he just isn't interested in gardens."

But Mrs. Tandy was worried, too.

Dave said, "At least the town of Enid is still there. Let's get going."

At the restaurant they talked to a friendly waitress.

She said, "Garden? You're looking for a beautiful garden?

"There's nothing like that in these parts ... unless ... I don't suppose you could mean a garden at the old Benson farm?"

30

Kathy jumped. "Benson? That's the name of the man who planted the garden we are looking for! Don't tell me the same family still owns it?"

The waitress nodded. "Yep. And I heard tell there used to be a fine garden there … gone wild ages ago, I bet.

"No one's gone up there for years. Except there's a caretaker they say. He farms it. Lives on the place. Kind of a hermit type, I guess.

"Even the Benson great-grandchildren ... no ... the great-great-great-grandchildren of the first owner ... don't go up there.

"They live here in town. Don't mix with the others much. But the Bensons still own it."

She filled Kathy's water glass and went on. "That farm brought shame to the family name years back. Don't know how. I only heard rumors.

"Nobody around here talks about it much anymore.

"The farm's twenty miles east of here, on County Road V.

"Want some more syrup for your waffles, honey?"

She put a pitcher down in front of Sammy, then went on with her work.

She warned them as they left, "Now careful on that road, it being springtime. It might be all mud."

So after feeding Mop his breakfast, off they went.

A few miles up the road, Dave said, "Look at this! Mud is right! You have to hit a wet patch at fifty miles an hour.

"By the time you pull out at the end, you're lucky to be going twenty!"

Bill said, "They sure had rain. Spring has sprung, all right."

That made Sammy think of flowers and the garden plans. He pulled the plans out of his pocket and looked them over.

After a minute he said, "Mr. Benson must have been one weird guy.

"Which I guess would explain why he changed his garden plan in the middle of a war."

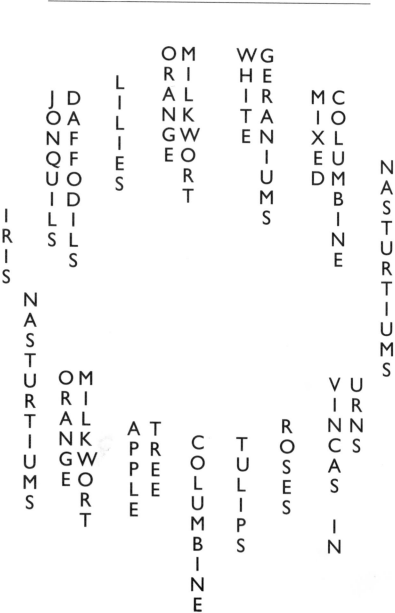

Dave looked at Sammy in the rearview mirror. He asked, "Why do you say that?"

Sammy said, "Look at this flower he listed! An orange milkwort!

"Now I KNOW there's no flower called a milkwort!

"He must have made that up. A wort is a bump that grows on your skin!"

Dave said, "Sammy, you're thinking of WART, not WORT. W-O-R-T means plant. It rhymes with HURT even though it looks like it would rhyme with SPORT.

"And W-A-R-T rhymes with SHORT, even though it's spelled like PART."

Sammy yelled, "HELP! STOP! You're mixing me up. And I still think orange milkwort is a funny name."

Kathy said, "Well, I think Sammy's right about Mr. Benson being a little strange.

"Orange milkwort is a wildflower. Why would he put a wildflower in a cutting garden?"

Now they all took out their garden plans for a closer look.

Mrs. Tandy said, "Well, come to think of it, why would he have planted that apple tree there?

"It's right in the middle of the flowers. It would give far too much shade."

Bill said, "Not only that, but he put his orange milkworts in two places, not just one. Right near each other.

"And he marked columbine and nasturtiums in two places, too."

Sammy said, "COL-um-bine? Nuh-STIR-shums? And look here! What kind of flowers are URNS?"

Dave said, "Urns are just big jars, usually made of stone."

Sammy said, "Well, that's another

weird thing. Why would he want urns in a cutting garden?"

Before they could answer that, they came to a split rail fence. Then they saw a mailbox. BENSON was written on it in faded black paint.

They turned in at the driveway. It led up a hill to an old, run-down, dark farmhouse.

Bill said, "This doesn't look too good. I don't see any garden."

Sammy said, "All I see is a gray house with its paint peeling."

Dave looked all around. "I don't see any caretaker, either."

Kathy whispered, "It looks scary."

Mrs. Tandy nodded.

Sammy said, "I'll go. I'm not scared."

But he dragged Bill out of the car with him.

Then he stood behind Bill. He pushed

Bill in front of him.

They went up the rotting steps to the patched-up front door.

They saw a door knocker shaped like a lion's head. A heavy iron ring hung from its mouth.

Sammy reached around Bill and knocked the ring against the door.

KNOCK! KNOCK!

They heard ... nothing.

Bill said, "I'll give it a try." He pounded the iron knocker HARD against the door.

BANG! BANG! BANG!

They heard an angry voice coming from around the back of the house.

"WHAT ARE YOU TRYING TO DO? BREAK DOWN THAT DOOR AGAIN? GET OFF THIS FARM!"

A man came around the corner.

He was tall and thin.

The skin on his tanned face looked rough as tree bark.

He was holding a shotgun.

Chapter 5:
The Missing Gold

Sammy looked sick.

His knees began to shake.

He grabbed Bill's arm.

Mrs. Tandy jumped out of the car.

She said, "Boys, come down off the porch. We are leaving."

The man stopped walking.

He looked at her. He stood the gun up against the house.

He said, "Oh, I'm sorry, ma'am. I didn't know it was a family.

"The gun's not loaded. I just carry it to scare off prowlers."

The man went on. "I've been away for a few days. Just returned this morning.

"I thought it was some strangers again, trying to break in. They've done it sixteen times since I've been here. And that's twenty-seven years now.

"I live here alone and farm the place myself.

"What can I do for you folks? You lost?"

Mrs. Tandy said, "Well, we may be

42

here on a fool's errand. But let's get the whole family out of the car. Then we can explain it to you."

First they let Mop out.

Then they got Dave's wheelchair. Dave and Kathy came over to talk.

Sammy said, "Boy, was Bill scared! He took one look at your gun and his knees turned to jelly!"

Bill poked him and said, "SAMMY! It was you I felt shaking, not me!"

Sammy poked Bill back and said, "Bill's always picking on me. I have to show him who's boss.

"Hey, do you want to know who we are?   The Woodlanders!   I'm Sammy Westburg and this is my best sister Kathy and my best friend Dave Briggs.

"And here's Mrs. Tandy, my other best friend. But you can call her Becky.

"And this is my brother Bill, my really

best friend.

"And this is our dog Mop, man's best friend."

The man laughed and said, "Well, howdy. I'm Jerome West. I see you have enough friends to last you a while. So what DO you folks need?"

Bill said, "Well, it's our vacation. We drove all the way down here from Bluff Lake to see a garden. But I guess we are out of luck."

Mr. West frowned. "What about a garden? You're not here to write a story about it, are you?

"Shame the Bensons? Start up the old rumors again?"

Dave said, "No. We heard there were rumors ... but not what the rumors were."

They told Mr. West the story of the book, and why they had come.

Then Bill asked, "Anyway, what made you think we were here to write a story?"

Mr. West said, "Because from time to time, someone does write one about the house. You see, this place has a history ... a sad history."

Then he told them this story:

"Well, you kids know about the Civil War, right? When Abe Lincoln was president?

"The north part of the United States

was fighting with the south part. Mostly about whether people should be able to keep slaves.

"The people in the South wanted the right to keep slaves.

"But many people in the North wanted the slaves to be set free. They were called the Union people.

"So anyway, the Bensons here were AGAINST slavery. They were for the Union army.

"But something happened that made the people around here think Mr. Benson was working against the Union."

Kathy asked, "What was it?"

Mr. West went on. "It was 1862, a year after the Civil War began.

"The Union people from around here wanted to help the Union army. So they collected their gold coins and family jewelry.

"They gave them to Mr. Benson so he could carry them north.

"But the next evening, Mr. Benson was found shot dead, not three miles away from this very farm.

"He never went to the North like he was supposed to. And he didn't have the gold on him.

"No one ever found out who shot him, either."

Mrs. Tandy said, "My heavens! This sounds like a story in a book! Please go on!"

He went on. "Mrs. Benson died of the flu a few days after her husband

47

was killed.

"And the gold was never seen again.

"Some folks whispered that Mr. Benson was seen sneaking around this farm ... the morning of the day he was killed.

"And some folks said he buried the gold here.

"And some folks said he gave the gold to his wife, and she stole it.

"But the worst was that some folks hinted that Mr. Benson GAVE the gold to the slave owners in the South to fight against the Union army.

"And just as bad, some folks said he just plain stole the gold. Put it in the bank. And they say it's in a bank box in the town of Enid to this day.

"You see, folks couldn't help wondering why he was back near his farm instead of a day's ride away, heading north."

Dave said, "I wonder, too, don't you?"

Mr. West frowned. "A lot of folks still want to believe that the gold has passed down through the Benson family.

"But I don't believe any of that talk! There aren't any nicer people than the Bensons in the whole town of Enid."

Mrs. Tandy shook her head sadly. She said, "Why, the poor family. They've had to wonder about Mr. and Mrs. Benson ever since ... not knowing if they were traitors, or thieves, or what."

Mr. West said, "Well, now you know everything I know ... except that one of Tom Benson's children found something.

"Just a few weeks after his dad's death, the son found a new plan for a cutting garden. Their father had drawn it.

"After the war the children planted it, to honor their parents.

"The children lived on here at the farm a few years, but their hearts were broken. They moved into town in the 1870s.

"The Benson family's lived there ever since. Good people, still trying to live down a terrible shame."

Sammy said, "Boy, is this a great mystery!

"But I hate it that the garden's gone. I would have loved to see it."

A slow smile lit up Mr. West's face.

He said, "Who says it's gone?"

Chapter 6:
Something's Wrong

Dave exclaimed, "You mean the garden's still here? After all these years?"

Mr. West said, "As a matter of fact, the garden WAS pretty well gone by the time I came here.

"Not much left.

"Just the oak grove ...

broken-down walls

the old stone garden house

the old brick paths

over-grown bushes and trees

cracked urns

... and starving flower beds thick with weeds.

"Just enough left to show what the garden had been like before."

Sammy asked, "How come no one took care of it?"

Mr. West said, "The other farmers who worked here through the years ... they didn't care much for gardening.

"But gardening is my great love.

"So just follow me and see what I made of it. It's right over on the other side of the hill."

He led them on a path that went around the house.

The Woodlanders could hardly believe their eyes.

Stretched out beneath them, in the middle of the cornfields, lay a huge and beautiful garden.

Sammy pulled out his garden plan.

He shouted, "Look! It's just like the drawing!

"There's the stone wall, and the opening to the path!"

The others crowded around his map.

Dave pointed. "There are the oak trees, way, way out there ... on the far right just where they're supposed to be."

Bill exclaimed, "Look, there's the fountain in the middle ... and it's working!"

53

Mr. West nodded. "It comes from a natural spring. The water shoots out of the ground without a pump."

Kathy said, "There, at the far end! The little house that's on the map!"

Mrs. Tandy pointed. "And look past the fountain, that maze, all made of bushes. Why, they must be six feet high, and shaped into solid walls!

"Mr. West, you must have worked every spare minute to bring this beautiful garden to life!"

Mr. West stood grinning for a minute.

Then he said, "Well, it doesn't leave me much time for doing much else. But it would be a lonely life here without my garden.

"And it sure is nice to be showing it off to people who like it."

Sammy shouted, "LIKE it! I LOVE it!

"I want to go walk in it.

54

"And play in the maze!

"And smell the flowers!"

By now he was jumping around, waving his arms. "I even wish I could LIVE here. I love farms. And you gave this one the best garden I ever saw!"

Sammy's hair was sticking out like old broom straws.

Bill poked him. He whispered, "Calm down, Sammy. You look like a hairy jumping bean. He will think you're rude."

But Mr. West laughed. "Sammy, I guess that's the nicest thing I've heard in twenty-seven years.

"Why, I wish you did live here. Say, how many days do you have for your vacation? Why not spend them here, on the farm? At the house?"

Kathy blushed. "Oh, Mr. West, I hope you don't think Sammy was asking you

55

to invite us!"

Mr. West smiled and said, "My good-ness, no. But I'm so lonely here, I wish you would stay.

"The house isn't much on the outside, but inside it's clean.

"And I have plenty of bedding stored away, crying to be used."

Mrs. Tandy said, "Mr. West, we couldn't just land on you and give you more work to do."

Bill said, "But ... maybe we could help you if we stayed.

"Is there anything we could do for you?"

Mr. West said, "Well, let's see. Do any of you happen to know how to cook? I haven't had a good home-cooked meal in years."

Sammy said, "Can we COOK? Mrs. Tandy's the best cook in Bluff Lake. Well, the universe.

"And we kids cook, too. We could make all your meals for you."

Dave asked, "What else could we do to help you?"

Mr. West thought for a minute. "Well, I keep a cow, so there's milking twice a day."

Kathy said, "We can do that! We all know how. And we can shovel manure to keep the barn clean."

Sammy added, "And we are GREAT at jumping from the bales of hay into a hay pile. And we can climb through tunnels between the bales!"

Bill poked him. "Sammy, that's not help!"

Mr. West laughed and said, "I've got all my fields planted. There's only the garden work left. Would you want to help with that?"

Kathy said, "Mr. West, there's nothing we would rather do."

Mr. West said, "Then that's it! Get your bags and follow me!"

The minute they entered the front door they knew they would love staying in that house.

Even Mop liked it. He ran around sniffing and barking.

The walls were as white as eggshells.

There were no curtains on the shiny clean windows. The Woodlanders looked out over the beautiful garden and farmland.

Mr. West led them to the back of the house.

He said, "The Bensons had a lot of kids. There are five bedrooms. Three are down here. I stay upstairs. Gives me a top view of my garden."

The boys wanted a room together.

They picked a big room downstairs with two double beds.

Bill said, "Sammy, you and I will be in one bed. But you stay on your side.

"You kick like a kangaroo."

Mrs. Tandy and Kathy took the room next to theirs.

They all un-packed in a hurry.

Then they followed Mr. West.

Mop ran next to them, through the kitchen, out the back door.

Then everybody helped Dave with his chair.

Carefully they took him down the hill and through an iron gate.

They were in the garden ... that beautiful garden ... at last.

But Sammy said, "Something's wrong."

Chapter 7:
Flowers, Flowers Everywhere

Sammy was looking at a brick wall twenty feet in front of them.

He said, "Wait a minute!

"Where's the maze?

"Where's the fountain?

"And the garden house?

"We could see them all from up on the hill."

They were standing between two rows of low-growing bushes. They saw beautiful beds of flowering plants beyond them ... and then the brick wall.

Bill said, "It doesn't look like the same garden from down here."

Mr. West explained, "The rest of the garden is behind that brick wall.

"The wall looks quite low when you're up above. But it's too tall to see over."

Dave said, "I see how it works. The garden is probably divided into lots of smaller gardens."

Mr. West nodded and began leading them forward ...

through a doorway in the wall

past bushes of every color of green
down stone steps and past a pond
through a tiny wild meadow
past a stone statue of a dog
past pink honeysuckle bushes

... and into a grassy place with brick walks, and trees clipped into animal shapes.

Sammy shouted, "Look, here's a dragon, and there's a horse!"

He ran from one tree to another.

In fact, he raced!

The others followed, trying to see every single tree.

Then Mr. West led them through an arbor made of thin strips of white-painted wood.

He said, "Grapes will be growing all over this arbor in a couple of months.

"And huge pink roses will bloom at each end."

63

They left the arbor and passed a brass sundial.

They came to a fountain. On stepping-stones they crossed a little stream that flowed from it.

Mr. West said, "This stream goes right past the garden house at the far end. That water's pure and clean."

They passed a statue of a boy in old-fashioned clothes.

And they saw flowers, flowers everywhere.

Mr. West said, "We sure are having a nice springtime this year. Everything's blooming early down here."

He began telling them some of the flower names. "This is foxglove. And monk's hood. And lilies and snapdragons. And bleeding heart."

Mrs. Tandy said, "You almost sound as if you were naming your children."

Mr. West smiled. "I AM naming my children. I have no family.

"So here are my kids! I'm like their

father ... I do what I can to help them grow. And I'm so proud of them when they do well!"

They followed a path to the left.

It led to one end of a solid wall of

bushes.

Dave said, "Hey, this must be the corner of the maze!"

Bill said, "Let's not go into the maze until later. Let's come here after lunch and check it out."

So they walked on past.

At last they came to the back end of the garden. They stopped at a big grove of giant oak trees.

In front of the grove stood a small, vine-covered, stone house.

A bird kept flying in and out of one of the windows.

Mrs. Tandy said, "I love this little house. Can we go inside?"

Dave said, "Does that bird have a nest in there? Will we scare her?"

Mr. West said, "Lands sake, no. I'm in and out of here every few days. The sparrow is used to traffic!

"Come right in!"

So they trooped in after him.

They saw a stone table with a stone bench on each side of it.

Another bench ran along one wall. A big black feather lay on the stone floor near it.

Mr. West said, "Well, how did that get in here? Didn't know a crow was using this place, too.

"Well, anyway, here's where the Benson children found a plan for the new cutting garden. Right on this stone table.

"There was a rock on it to keep it

from blowing away.

"I'll show you that cutting garden on the way back to the house."

Sammy said, "It's lucky the kids even found the new plan. You'd think Mr. Benson would have thought of a safer place to keep it."

Kathy thought for a minute. "Well, maybe he liked to work on it while he was sitting out here in the oak grove. Maybe he kept adding to it when he got new ideas."

Bill said, "Then you'd think he'd just keep it with him. Then he could write stuff on it whenever he wanted."

Sammy said, "Yep. Out here a mouse could have eaten it."

Mr. West asked, "Say, would you like to see that original plan, in Mr. Benson's own hand-writing?"

Dave said, "WOULD we! It would be

like holding a piece of Civil War history in our hands!"

Mr. West said, "Remind me when we go back to the house. I'll get it out. It's in a tea can on the shelf. Right above the fireplace.

"In fact, let's head back now. We can walk past the fruit orchard and end up at the cutting garden. We can even cut a bloom or two for the table."

Mrs. Tandy said, "And the great Woodland Cooks will roll up their sleeves and make lunch for you!"

They came to the apple orchard.

Mr. West said, "There are some good old trees here, perfect for climbing. Be my guest!"

In a second, Kathy, Mrs. Tandy, Bill, and Sammy were in the trees.

Mop raced from tree to tree, hopping on his hind legs, trying to follow them

69

up.

Dave called up at them, "You climbed up there like four squirrels!"

Sammy shouted, "I'm not a squirrel. They're the squirrels! I'm Superman!

"And now I'm coming on down. I want to go see the other stuff!"

But just then Kathy called out, "Wait a second!"

She was pointing over the orchard wall. "What's that?"

Chapter 8: Anna Benson

Bill, Sammy, and Mrs. Tandy stared at where Kathy was pointing.

From up in their trees they could see much more of the garden.

Bill said, "What did you see, Kathy?"

Kathy shook her head. "I don't know. I thought I saw something out of the corner of my eye ... moving ... over there."

Mrs. Tandy said, "You mean near the maze bushes, honey? I don't see anything there now."

Kathy said, "I guess maybe I was just seeing things."

They climbed down from their trees.

But Sammy was worried. He said, "But how about a prowler?

"How about a bank robber? Or someone who escaped from jail? Or a crazy person? Or a runaway hiding in the maze?"

Mr. West laughed. "Then I'd feel sorry for that person. That maze is HUGE. And it's tricky. A prowler would get lost in there in about a second.

"I clip the bushes that form the maze myself. I've done it all these years, and I still get mixed up in it.

"One day last year I lost track of where I was. Took me half an hour to find my way out of it."

Dave said, "I know what you mean. We have copies of the plan for the maze. I have trouble following it, even on paper."

Mr. West got a faraway look on his face. He said, "Only person I ever knew who could make any sense out of it was one of the Benson kids. Anna Benson was her name.

"Funny little kid.

"Wild black hair.

"Great big nose.

"Chin too big.

"Chubby as an apple.

"She was really interested in her

family's story. That was back twenty-five years ago. She was just ten.

"She and her mother stayed at the farm with me one whole summer."

Sammy said, "Those lucky guys!"

Mr. West went on.

"I'd already spent two years working on the garden by then ... I already had some pretty wonderful flowers growing round and about.

"Anna brought the old cutting garden map here from town. She put it in the tea can it's still in."

Bill asked, "Why did she bring it here?"

Mr. West said, "She thought the map was a code message.

"She spent every single night looking at that paper.

"She spent every day digging in that cutting garden for the gold. She just had

74

to prove that her great-great-great-grandparents weren't crooks.

"But she never found a thing.

"Well, after all, she was only ten."

Sammy said, "ONLY TEN? What do you mean, she was only ten?

"That's just how old I am!"

He pulled himself up straight as a fence post. He said, "Look at me! Ten isn't so little. I'm only one inch shorter than Bill, and he's fourteen!

"And I weigh just as much.

"And my brain is just as big … probably bigger!"

Bill just grinned.

75

Sammy went on. "And I think the map IS a clue to the gold.

"In fact, I KNOW it is!

"So where is this Anna person now? Why doesn't she keep on looking?"

Mr. West answered, "I sure didn't mean to insult you ten-year-olds, Sammy. Anna was a darling thing, the apple of my eye.

"I was twenty-two years old, but I loved being with her. I couldn't help wishing she were my sister.

"But her folks got divorced that year. Her mother took her off to Europe. That was the end of that."

Sammy said, "Well, it shouldn't have been the end of that. Because she was RIGHT!"

He had his mad-dog detective look on his face.

He stuck out his jaw.

His eyes were half-shut.

He wrinkled his nose.

He made his hands into fists.

He turned to Bill and said, "You think she was right, don't you, Bill? If you don't, you're a big creep!"

Bill said, "Calm down, Sammy. I DO think she was right ... but not just because you look ready to punch me."

Dave said, "Me, too, Sammy. And I think I know why Mr. Benson left the map in the garden house.

"I don't think he was keeping it there to work on it.

"I think he drew it in a hurry.

"He probably left it for someone to find ... right when he found out the gold ... and his life ... were in danger.

"He probably left it as a message showing where he hid the gold."

Kathy said, "But Dave, we've looked at

our copies over and over. We haven't spotted any coded messages."

Dave said, "But our copies are from the book. The map we saw was set in type.

"Maybe there was something different about the way Mr. Benson drew it. Let's go back and take a look at the map in his own hand-writing!"

They made a dash for the house.

Chapter 9: Is It a Code?

They moved Dave's chair so fast, it bounced all the way.

They rushed him up the steps into the house.

Mr. West walked over to the fireplace in the living room. He took down a tin box with flowers printed all over it. On one side was the word TEA.

In it was a roll of paper.

Carefully he spread it open on the table.

Sammy said, "Man, this Thomas Benson had really messy hand-writing! He should have had a computer!"

Mr. West said, "Now that I think of it, that's a funny thing.

"I saw a letter Mr. Benson wrote once. One of the present-day Bensons showed it to me. He had BEAUTIFUL hand-writing."

Kathy said, "Maybe that goes along with what Dave said. Maybe he wrote this in a big hurry."

Bill leaned over the table. "Let's try to figure this out!"

Sammy said, "How about if all the first letters make a message? Let's go around the circle. But where would we start?"

Dave said, "Start anywhere. Let's see if any words turn up. Here, I'll start at the top and go clock-wise."

He wrote on the back of his own copy:

W-G-m-C-N-U-V-R-T-C-T-A-m-O-N-I-J-D-L-O-m

Sammy watched as Dave wrote.

He said, "I don't see a single word in that message except TAM. That's a hat. He sure didn't hide the gold in a tam. I guess my idea stinks."

Sammy looked so sad that Bill said, "It was a good idea anyway, Sammy. Maybe there's a message if we read it the other way."

Bill wrote this:

G-W-m-O-L-O-J-I-n-O-m-A-T-C-T-R-V-U-n-e-m

Sammy said, "Look! There are the words MOLD and IN and MAT!

"Do you think he hid it under a moldy mat somewhere? But why would you hide something under a moldy mat?"

Kathy pointed. "But ... look, all the letters for the word GOLD and the word IN are there.

"But you'd have to use the G. Then you'd have to skip the W and M. Then you'd use the O and L and D. Then you'd have to skip the J. No real pattern."

Mrs. Tandy said, "Well ... all the letters for the word ATTIC are there, but they're all mixed up."

Sammy added, "And there are almost all the letters for the word LUNCH!

"I bet the message means that we should look for the gold in the mixed-up

82

attic after lunch!

"So let's make lunch! I'm STARVED!"

Kathy said, "That's a good idea, Sammy. Then let's go look at the maze.

"Sometimes when you're trying to figure things out, you should stop for a while. Then your brain works on the problem without your even knowing it!"

Dave said, "It's a good plan. Let's check out the kitchen."

They found five boxes of cookies ... thick cream, milk, flour, eggs, and butter ... canned peaches ... and an old waffle iron.

They ended up making waffles for lunch ... but Sammy hardly helped.

He kept running in and out of the kitchen.

So the others chopped up the peaches.

They whipped the cream.

Mrs. Tandy put the peaches and

whipped cream on top of the double waffles.

They shouted for Sammy, and sat down to eat.

Mr. West REALLY dived in.

First he ate one double waffle.

Then he ate a single one.

Then he had two more double ones.

Then Dave made him another single.

Sammy said, "Mr. West, you're as thin as a giraffe. But you eat waffles like an elephant."

Bill and Kathy poked him, but that didn't stop him.

He went on. "Four double waffles is even more than I can eat. You must have been starving!"

Mr. West laughed and said, "I was starving … for good home cooking. I'm going to love having you here.

"And I think you'd all better call me Jerry instead of Mr. West.

"And may I call you Becky, Mrs. Tandy?"

Sammy giggled

He whispered to Bill, "They say the way to the heart is through the stomach. Here's the proof. Four double waffles and Mrs. T. has a new boyfriend."

Mrs. Tandy smiled, "Of course you should call me Becky!" She looked over at Sammy and said, "If my main boy friend, Sammy here, doesn't mind."

Sammy turned red. He jumped up and said, "Let's clean up fast. Then let's go out to the maze.

"But I get to wash the dishes. I HATE to dry!"

By the time they got out to the maze it was 3:00.

Jerry said, "Here we are! Well, I have a few things to do, so why don't you go in without me?"

Sammy said, "No problem! We are the maze MASTERS!"

Mr. West smiled. "That may be, but you should still stick together. Then you won't worry if you get lost.

"How long do you want to spend

here? I'll come back and hunt you down whenever you say."

Dave said, "How about an hour or two, guys? What if Jerry comes for us around four-thirty or five?"

They all agreed.

Jerry said, "I'll come back and give a holler. If you're lost inside somewhere I'll come through and pick you up."

Sammy ran off a little way. He called, "I'm out of here. I'll meet you slowpokes later.

"I'm starting from the other end. I've got my map. And my compass. Good-BYE! And don't follow me, Bill!"

He darted off across the front of the maze and around the right-hand corner toward the back of the garden. M o p ran along beside him.

Bill gasped, "I'm going with him. He might get lost and scared. He's ALWAYS doing stuff like this."

He took off running. He yelled, "SAMMY! SAMMY! Wait up!"

But by the time Bill got to the far opening in the maze, Sammy was deep inside, alone.

Chapter 10:
Lost in the Maze

Sammy ran down the gravel path of the first row of the maze.

He turned right into a cross row.

The solid green wall of bushes stood

high above his head.

The sky looked as blue as a robin's egg.

Small perfect clouds hung over him.

Sammy whispered to himself, "I bet old Bill follows me. I'm not going to let him catch up for a while. I'll hide. Then I'll jump out and scare him!"

He took a few more turns in the maze.

Then he remembered his map.

He took it out of his pocket to find out exactly where he was.

He saw the corner where he had entered. Then he realized something. He didn't remember what turns he had taken!

On the map he tried to find the last opening he'd come through.

He ran back to check on it, but it wasn't where he remembered it.

From somewhere Bill called, "Sammy, where are you? Are you lost?"

That made Sammy mad.

He shouted back, "What do you mean, lost? Of COURSE not! I'm fine!

"Why don't you leave me alone?

"Mop and I are having a good time.

"And we've gone into a hiding place so you won't find us!

"And I don't want to talk anymore, so just scram!"

Bill said, "Well, then, I'll see if I can walk through and find the others. Call me if you need me!"

Sammy shouted, "Good-bye, pest!"

He listened for Bill's answer.

He listened for Bill's footsteps. He heard a faint crunching ... feet walking on the maze's gravel path.

But the leafy walls of the maze killed most of the sound.

He tried to hear where Bill was now.

He said aloud, "Good.   He's gone.
I'm alone. At last! Now I'll find my way
back before Bill does."

He kept walking down the gravel
path.

After a while he said to Mop, "Stay
near me, Moppy. I don't want you to get
scared. Come this way."

He walked around a few more turns
in the maze.

Suddenly he realized Mop wasn't with him.

"MOP! MOPPY!"

He heard Mop bark in answer, but he couldn't see him.

Then he realized Mop's bark came from the other side of the bushes. Mop had somehow gotten into the next row!

Sammy turned back. He kept calling, "Come on, Mop!"

He got to the end of the row. There was an opening into another row ... but it was on the side AWAY from Mop's bark.

Sammy went through it anyway.

By the time he found another opening he could hear only a faint bark.

He called, "Mop! Mop! Here, Mop!"

But Mop didn't come.

He didn't bark, either.

Sammy was alone ... lost in that

huge maze.

He said to himself, "Oh, well. Bill or Jerry will find me. Let's see. I think the front of the garden is to the west. So I'll just keep following the sun."

But suddenly the world grew dark.

Sammy looked up.

The little white clouds had blown away.

The sky was one big scary dark gray sheet.

Sammy couldn't even see the sun. Then he remembered his compass.

He pulled it out of his pocket. He figured out which direction was west.

He started walking again.

But he came to the end of the row he was in and found ... a dead end.   There was no opening at all!

A few drops of rain splashed on his face.   Then rain poured down.

Sammy whispered, "I'm in for it now. I'm not just going to get wet, I'm going to get SOAKED!"

Then he heard the crunch of gravel.

He shouted, "Bill!   Hey, Bill!   Oh, B-i-i-i-i-l-l!   ANSWER ME, BILL!"

But nobody answered.

Sammy looked at his watch.

He said softly, "Good grief.   It's only four-fifteen.   Jerry might wait till five before he comes for us!

"And maybe Bill won't show up because I called him a pest.

"I'm wet and cold.

"My shoes are soaked.

"My socks are squishy.

"I'm lost and I've lost MOP.

"It's scary and I feel trapped.

"Everyone will be mad at me."

And then ... Sammy saw something that made him feel a lot better.

Lying on its side on the path was a ladder. He stood it up. It was about as tall as the walls of the maze.

He climbed the ladder and stood on the very top. He shouted, "Hello? Bill? You guys can come and get me now!"

He stretched up on his tip-toes.

He waved his arms ... so someone might have a better chance of seeing him.

And then ... he lost his balance and FELL!

Chapter 11: The Stranger

Sammy fell onto the top of the wall of
bushes ...

    then halfway down through them

    then out the other side

then into the next row of the maze ... and then into the arms of a woman!

She tried to hold on to him, but he dropped to the ground. He landed flat on his back, but he wasn't hurt at all.

The woman looked half-worried, and half-smiling. She noticed his T-shirt and said, "That wasn't your best landing, Superman."

Sammy stared up from where he was.

He saw she had a biggish nose.

And a biggish chin.

She was as chubby as an apple.

She had wild black hair sticking out in every direction, with a big blue jay feather stuck in it.

She said, "Are you all right?"

Sammy said, "Sure. I'm tough. But how about you? I came down pretty hard. Thanks for catching me.

"I hope I didn't hurt you ... but who

are you? Should you be here? Are you a bank robber?

"And what about that feather?

"Hey, were you sneaking around this garden a couple of hours ago?

"I bet you were the one my sister Kathy saw moving around near this maze. Were you?

"Wait until Jerry West sees you! He's going to be MAD!"

The stranger jumped. "JERRY WEST! You don't mean to say Jerry West still runs this farm!"

Sammy said, "Yes, and he sure will give you a real hard time if he catches you. You better scram, and fast.

"He should be here in about fifteen minutes, maybe."

The woman said, "Well, I'm NOT scramming. I want to meet this scary Jerry West. So let's go find him."

Sammy shook his head. "We can't! I'm lost!

"And my four friends are probably lost, too! And I lost my dog!

"I have a map, but I can't figure it out. See, here's where I want to go, to this front corner."

The woman said, "I see. I can figure it out. Follow me."

She led the way back and forth and side to side through the maze.

In a little while they heard Mop's bark.

The woman led Sammy to the row Mop was in.

Sammy hugged him so hard, Mop yipped a little.

Finally Sammy came out at the front corner of the maze. The woman stayed back, just inside the maze.

Everybody was standing there together.

Sammy said, "How come you got out so soon?"

Bill said, "We couldn't have without Jerry."

Dave added, "We were so lost, we never made it to the back of the maze."

Mrs. Tandy said, "Jerry got here early and fished us out. You saved us, didn't you, Jerry?"

But Jerry West didn't answer.

He was staring at the woman walking out of the maze.

Then he gasped just two words, "Little Anna?"

The woman answered, "Jerry? After twenty-five years? Is it really you?"

They ran toward each other.

They hugged like two wrestlers.

Then Jerry held her off to look at her again.

He said, "Still picking up bird feathers and wearing them in your hair, I see!

"Folks, remember the little girl I told you about? Little Anna Benson? This is that little girl, come back!"

She laughed and said, "Not so little, Jerry, and older!

"I'm finally back in Indiana to take up my gold hunt again.

"I haven't even seen my relatives in town yet.

"I was afraid they'd think I was crazy to be doing this."

Jerry said, "How long have you been around here?"

Anna said, "Two days. I've been sleeping in the garden house and looking for clues in the cutting garden."

Jerry said softly, "The crow's feather...

in the stone house."

Anna went on. "This morning was the first time I heard anyone else around. So I ran for the maze.

"I never dreamed it would be you, that you'd still be here, Jerry."

Jerry said, "And I never dreamed you'd come back ... or even remember me!"

Anna said, "How could I ever forget you? The summer I spent here was the happiest summer of my life!

"After we went to Europe I finished school and studied art.

"I've been a college teacher for years. I taught painting in England. And I took care of my mother. She was sick for a long time.

"She never would come back to the United States, so I didn't, either.

"But this year my mother died."

Jerry said, "I'm so sorry. She was a

lovely person."

Anna said, "I began painting again. I started to paint pictures of flowers. Then I began a picture of what I thought was a make-believe garden.

"One day I took a good look at my picture. I realized it wasn't make-believe. It was THIS garden, MY garden. YOUR garden.

"I never knew I was thinking about it all through the years.

"I asked for a leave of absence from my teaching. And I finally came home. Something told me I HAD to.

"And here I am.

"And here I'll start the search again.

"And here I'll clear the shadow from my family's name.

"And here I may stay ... forever."

Dave said, "We'd like to help solve the mystery if you need us."

Anna looked at the Woodlanders' eager faces. "NEED you! Do flowers need sunlight?"

She smiled at Sammy. "Does the world need Superman? Of course I need you!"

Jerry kept looking at Anna and grinning from ear to ear.

Sammy poked Mrs. Tandy and said, "Uh-oh, Mrs. T. It looks like you're losing your new boyfriend!"

Mrs. Tandy gave him a little hug and whispered, "That's OK, honey. As long as I still have you!"

Then she turned to Anna and said, "Well, what are we waiting for? Let's go take a look at that MAP!"

A second later they were dashing toward the house again.

Chapter 12:
Cracking the Code

They raced inside.

Jerry took down the tea can.

He reached in for the rolled-up map.

He cried, "IT'S GONE!"

Sammy said, "Don't worry. I hid it. I figured if Kathy thought she saw someone outside today, then she did.

"Kathy's as shy as a bird, but she's as smart as a fox!

"I was afraid a prowler was hanging around to steal the map!"

Bill smiled. "Why, you little sneak! So that's why you kept running in and out of the kitchen at lunchtime. So where's the map?"

Sammy ran over to the piano. He lifted the top of the piano bench. But there was nothing there but old sheet music.

His face fell.

He said, "This is where I put it! There was room for the roll right here in the corner. Oops, now I remember. I moved it ... to behind this picture."

He lifted a picture. No map.

He started darting around the room. "Let me see ... I got afraid the picture too heavy ... it might flatten a rolled-up paper ...

"So I put it in that green glass vase ... but you could see the map through it ... so then I took it out and put it behind this couch pillow ... but it isn't here."

He looked plenty worried.

Suddenly Anna ran over to the fireplace.

She picked up a white pottery dog sitting against the brick wall.

She turned it upside-down. She looked inside the hollow bottom and grinned.

"Here it is!" she called.

Sammy said, "Now I remember putting it there! How did you know?"

Anna said, "Because I used to hide things inside him myself, when I was ten.

Now, let's sit around the kitchen table and brainstorm."

They crowded around the old map.

Suddenly Dave said, "Wait! I see something weird! I see it on THIS map, but not on the copies we made from the book!

"Look, every time Mr. Benson wrote two words together, he started one higher than the other. Was it because he was in a hurry?

"Or did he mean to use only one word from each pair? Maybe just the lower words. NO! I SEE IT! It's the HIGHER ones, plus the single words!

"The first letter of each. Hey, Bill, let's see that code you wrote down!"

Bill handed him his copy. Dave looked at the map and crossed out all the lower words.

Bill shouted, "Gold in oak trunk!"

ORANGE MILKWORT

WHITE GERANIUMS

MIXED COLUMBINE

DAFFODILS

LILIES

JONQUILS

NASTURTIUMS

IRIS

NASTURTIUMS

URNS

VINCAS IN

ROSES

TULIPS

COLUMBINE

APPLE TREE

ORANGE MILKWORT

NASTURTIUMS

G-O-LD-O-L-D-F-I-n-O-DY-A-T-C-T-R-A-U-n-C-AT

Sammy shouted, "Boy, this guy sure spells weird!"

Jerry exclaimed, "Oak trunk! I know where there's an oak trunk! An old one, too! Stored away in the attic! Follow me!"

He grabbed a flashlight, a hammer, and a screwdriver.

They ran after him to the stairs.

They all helped carry Dave up in his chair. Mop danced up the steps in front of them.

The attic was a mess.

Boxes. Baskets of Christmas ornaments. Bags of papers. Piles of old farm tools and magazines. Racks of old clothes. Pieces of broken furniture.

Sammy looked around and groaned, "I don't see a trunk."

Jerry said, "Don't worry. The trunk's

in a storeroom behind that door."

He pointed to a wide, low door.

He said, "That door opens into the slanting part under the roof."

He opened it. Mop sniffed. Then slowly he sneaked in.

Dave wheeled in after him. He called

to the others, "Bend down so you don't bump your heads."

They hurried in after Dave.

Jerry aimed the flashlight at a huge old wooden trunk.

He said, "It's locked and there's no key. I never felt I had the right to break into it. Anyway, it seemed empty. It's pretty light-weight."

Anna said, "Well, you have the right to open it now. Open away!"

Jerry hammered the screwdriver under the trunk's big brass lock. Finally the lock flew up.

Anna lifted the lid.

They all stared inside.

They saw … nothing.

Nothing at all.

Then Kathy said, "Well, you know I've read about false bottoms in old trunks. You don't think … "

Quick as a wink Bill felt around inside. In a minute he found a small spring sticking up from the bottom.

He wiggled it. He felt something snap into place.

He pulled up on the spring.

Slowly he lifted out a false trunk bottom.

They stared inside again.

THEY SAW ... nothing.

Sammy groaned. "Rotten rats! Now what?"

Dave said, "Jerry, is there another oak trunk?"

Jerry shook his head. "I'm afraid not."

Anna said sadly, "Then that's that. Thanks, all of you, for trying to help. But this could be the end of the trail."

Slowly they went downstairs.

Mrs. Tandy said, "I'll make us some

tea. Maybe that will perk us up."

Kathy patted Anna's shoulder. She said softly, "I hope you didn't come all the way from England for nothing."

But Anna smiled. She said, "Oh, no. Not for nothing.

"I've come back to my real home. I found it more beautiful than I remembered it.

"And I met all of you!"

Then Sammy blurted out, "And you found Jerry here, waiting! And you should see the way he looks at you!"

Chapter 13:
Another Oak Trunk!

Bill, Kathy, Dave, and even Mrs. Tandy
poked Sammy at the same time.

He squeaked like a mouse.

He ran around the table.

He said, "How come you guys are always poking me? I'm just saying what you're all thinking.

"Maybe she was a little girl when she went away ... but she's grown up now. And Jerry LIKES her!"

Anna laughed.   She ran over to Sammy.

She put her arms around him.   Her dark eyes darted from one person to another.   She looked like a mother chicken protecting her baby chick.

She said, "Don't poke this darling child. I love what he says."

Jerry grinned and said, "So do I. He's just about perfect!"

Sammy stuck out his tongue so far at Bill it hurt.

Just then they heard the tea kettle whistle.

Mrs. Tandy said, "Well, now, our tea is ready!"

She brought a tray of tea to the table.

She filled a giant bowl with cookies and brought it to them.

She said, "I was thinking while the water was boiling.

"I can't believe Mr. Benson left that note for his wife for no reason.

"I can't believe there was no gold hidden ... somewhere.

"Why don't we take our tea back to

the old garden house. We can sit there and think this through again. Or let's sit out under the oaks back there.

"Let's brainstorm some more."

Suddenly Dave shouted, "Wait! Forget the tea, Mrs. T.! And every one COME ON! FAST! To the far end of the garden!"

So Bill and Sammy rushed Dave out of the house ... down the hill ... through the front gardens ... past the maze garden ... and over toward the garden house.

Dave yelled, "Keep going, into that bunch of oak trees over there!

"Don't you see? They're OAK TREES! Oak trees have OAK TRUNKS!

"GOLD IN OAK TRUNK!

"The gold's GOT to be in a hole in one of these trees!"

Everyone ran among the trees.

But if Dave was right, which tree?

They searched the whole oak grove, tree by tree.

They couldn't find even one with a big enough hole in it.

Finally Sammy said, "Well, I give up. There isn't any dumb gold.

"If one of these trees ever had a hole in it, it closed up."

Jerry shook his head.

He said, "Not likely, Sammy. A little lost bark would heal over, but a hole would stay open. It would rot out even more as the years passed."

Sammy walked over to a huge old fallen tree. He sat down on the hollow trunk.

Jerry sat down next to him, and Anna sat with them.

Before the three of them could say a word, Dave wheeled over to them.

Kathy and Bill rushed right along with him.

Dave grabbed a branch from the ground. He handed it to Kathy. He pointed at a big opening in the hollow trunk.

She poked the branch into it.

She dragged it back out through the soft, rotten wood.

Out came a spider.

Out came a cricket.

Out came a centipede and some ants and a beetle.

And out came something shiny, on the end of Kathy's stick.

It was a gold necklace.

Bill shouted, "You DID it, Dave! You found the oak trunk!"

Sammy looked at the insects running all around it. "Ugh!" he said.

Then he looked at the necklace.

The next minute he dived head-first into the rotten trunk.

A second later he backed out fast, like a sports car out of a garage.

Everyone tried to brush him off.

He held out his hands. They were full of dust and leaves and a big white grub and ... an antique gold pin and bracelet and coin.

Sammy puffed dust out of his nose. He blew off a piece of leaf sticking to his lip. But he was grinning.

He said, "There's a lot more in there, but some bugs tried to kill me."

Dave said, "Sammy, you did a great job. We can chop into this trunk and get the rest out later.

"Poor Mr. Benson. He died trying to keep the gold safe. He must have found out he was being followed. He knew he might be killed for the gold.

"So he made the map in code for his wife. They must have used this same code before. But she was sick, and she died before she could read it."

Anna started to cry. She sniffled, "I just knew Thomas Benson didn't steal his neighbors' jewelry."

Sammy said, "No wonder it looked like such a weird plan for a cutting garden. It was only a secret message. He never expected it to be planted.

"But his kids didn't know that, and

planted it!

"Anyway, the garden looks pretty good for a huge mistake!"

Anna sniffled again. "If they hadn't planted it, the map might never have been saved."

Jerry put his arms around her.

He said, "Come on, Anna. Don't cry anymore. I'll get the reporter from the Enid newspaper here tomorrow.

"By this time next week, everyone will know what a brave man Thomas Benson really was."

Sammy said, "And boy, Anna, you're super-rich!"

Anna shook her head. "Oh, no. I earn enough money to take care of myself. And the gold isn't really mine.

"It came from families all around. But how can I give it back to the real owners? They're all long dead."

Dave said, "You could start a museum for Enid, with the gold in it. Then everyone could enjoy it."

Anna smiled and said, "That's a fine idea!"

Bill said, "This calls for a party! You all wait in the garden house. Come on, Sammy!"

He and Sammy ran all the way back to the farmhouse.

In a few minutes they came running back.

Bill was carrying a big plastic pitcher of iced tea.

Sammy had the cookies and paper cups in a bag.

The Woodlanders and their new friends sat down around the stone table.

They ate cookies dunked in cool tea.

They laughed and talked.

Even Mop munched away.

A bird flew in and picked up the cookie crumbs.

Sammy noticed Jerry and Anna holding hands under the table.

He grinned and said, "You know, Anna, the garden would be a perfect place for a wedding."

And nobody poked him.